The Perfect Christmas Tree

WRITTEN BY

Michael Pellico

ILLUSTRATED BY

Malane Newman

See more children's books at MoonbowPublishing.com

First Print Edition
ISBN 978-1-7339130-6-5
Library of Congress Control Number: 2020916357
Printed in USA

This book is dedicated to:

Sabrina Pellico

The inspiration for this story... and many others.

And to my mother:

Helen Pellico

My hero and guiding light throughout my life.

It was a beautiful forest. Many different kinds of trees grew there: Oak, Redwood, Maple, Dogwood and White Pine. However, the forest was mostly pine trees—the trees we know as Christmas Trees.

In the North were tall, snowed covered mountains. In the West was a green valley, with colorful wildflowers that made the valley look like a bright, colorful carpet every spring. This was the home of deer, fox, rabbits, owls, eagles, badgers, skunks, bears, and raccoons. Beavers lived by the clear, cold creek where trout and bass called home.

In the middle of the forest, there was a grove full of young Christmas Trees. It was a beautiful early spring day and a tall Christmas Tree was talking. He was the father of all the pine trees around him.

"Look around," the Christmas Tree said, in a deep voice that was carried by the wind. "Do you see the stumps? Do you know what happened to those trees? Our missing friends? They were once wonderful trees—tall, straight and very proud of their beauty. That was their downfall."

"At the end of every year, humans come to our forests with saws and axes. These humans have a holiday they call Christmas. For this holiday, humans chop down our friends and put them on top of their cars or trucks and bring them home, where they cover them with lights, decorations, and tinsel."

"Sadly we never see them again. So this year we have a plan. I want you all to grow up UGLY! Grow crooked, bent, twisted, skinny, both fat and skinny, and lots of bare spots. And did I already say ugly? Yes, ugly! Only by doing that, can you save yourselves from becoming Christmas Trees!"

All the young trees listened attentively, each planning how to be the ugliest tree in the forest. Except a young tree called "Little Stevie". He was a very proud little tree and was determined to be the most beautiful tree in the forest.

"No Little Stevie! Do not grow up handsome. Please listen to Father," pleaded one of his sisters called Sabrina. "You know Father is right. We must grow up as ugly as we can. You can see the stumps left by our friends," she said, pointing to the stumps around them.

"Aw, I am not afraid. Besides, Father is fooling us because he wants to be the tallest, strongest and best looking tree. What a silly story anyway, Christmas Trees!"

"Ha ha!" Sabrina said. "Do not be so proud. You must listen to Father. He may be tall and very handsome, but he loves all of us and is trying to warn and protect us!"

Little Stevie would not listen and despite his father and Sabrina's begging, he kept growing straight and tall with strong branches. All the other trees looked at him with admiration, wondering if he was smart not to listen to their father. Sabrina, however, looked sad and worried. "I hope you will be okay," Sabrina said. "Father had always tried to be a good father. He never really cared if he was handsome and was never jealous of the other trees."

It was almost the end of the year and the forest was soon covered with snow. The other trees, except for the pine trees, had lost their leaves. The pine trees were the only trees that looked green. They were green but ugly! Everywhere you looked there were pine trees bent and twisted! Their branches were crooked and went in every direction! Except for one tree.

There, in the center of all the ugly trees, was Little Stevie.

Standing tall, with a perfect shape and branches straight and thick, Little Stevie was a beautiful pine tree. All the other pine trees began to question whether they should have listened to their father. Maybe they should have grown up beautiful too.

Only Sabrina disagreed. "Our father was right that being ugly will save us from being cut down. It does not matter how we look if we are healthy and strong and are wonderful homes for birds to build their nests. Look around. We are still bright green. Father is smart and knows what will protect us.

"Ha ha," Little Stevie laughed. "That is a silly story Father told us. Look at me. How beautiful am I? Such a silly story."

Sabrina shook her branches in sadness, she knew and trusted her father and worried about her vain brother who refused to listen.

The snow storms were coming more frequently now and the ground was covered with a thick cover of powdery snow. On the little creek, there was even a thin lay of ice. Everything was peaceful in the forest.

One morning there was a huge commotion, as hundreds of birds flew into the air shouting, "The humans are coming. The humans are coming!"

Sabrina called up to the birds, "Are many coming?"

An owl swooped down, “Yes many, and they are carrying saws and axes.”

Sabrina could see the animals moving deeper into the forest, away from the oncoming humans. All the pine trees were talking, “I hope we are ugly enough so they leave us alone.”

They nervously looked at each other. Then, they suddenly looked at Little Stevie. He stood there not saying anything but trembled in fear.

"I'm so scared. What is going to happen to me? Father, Father help me! I do not want to be cut down. I love the forest and want to stay here with my family and all my animal friends."

His father looked sad, "I warned you. There is nothing I can do now Little Stevie."

You could hear the human children talking and they were not happy, "These are the ugliest trees we have ever seen! Look at how crooked and bent they are. Look at the branches. We cannot hang lights or ornaments on them. Why did we come here?"

"Wait! Look over there! I see a perfect Christmas Tree!" a little boy pointed at Little Stevie. Children and their parents started walking excitedly towards Little Stevie.

"Oh no! They have seen me!" Shaking in fear, Little Stevie did not know what he could do. All the other trees were sad but felt helpless to help.

"Are you happy now Little Stevie? Are you happy that you are so beautiful?" Little Stevie heard a voice say.

Looking down, Little Stevie saw a very short old man. He had a very long brown beard that touched his toes. You could see that it touched his toes because he was not wearing any shoes! His toe nails were long and curled up. The little man was dressed in clothes that looked like leaves, and his arms looked strangely like branches!

"Well did you learn your lesson?" asked the little man.

"Oh yes!" cried Little Stevie, "I should have listened to my father! He is so smart and I was vain trying to show off."

The little man asked, "Did being beautiful make you happier? Did you have more friends?"

"No" Little Stevie said sadly. Now it was too late. Turning to his father, Little Stevie said, "Father I am sorry for not listening to you. I am sorry I let you down and for not being a good son. Sabrina, you were right. I will miss you and everyone. I hope everyone learns from my foolishness."

"Well, well. I believe you have learned your lesson!" the little man laughed. Taking an old, brown bag off his back, he opened the strings and took out a jar. Opening the jar and using his hand, he scooped out a glob that looked like black sticky tar. He quickly rubbed the sticky tar on the trunk of Little Stevie.

Little Stevie started to shake rapidly. In amazement, they watched as he started to bend and twist. His branches began losing pine needles and some of his branches fell off.

Within minutes, Little Stevie looked like the other pine trees! Sabrina and the other trees looked at Little Stevie, "Wow you look just like us!"

"Thank you," Sabrina said to the little man. But he was not there. Where he had been standing, there was a large hole. He must live underground.

Very soon the children and their parents arrived. "Where is that beautiful tree?" they cried in disappointment. "It was right here—not this ugly tree." pointing at Little Stevie. "This is not a forest of beautiful Christmas Trees. Let us go to another forest." They turned and slowly walked back to their cars and trucks.

The trees watched them go, and as soon as the humans were away, they started laughing and talking happily.

Little Stevie was the happiest. “We may be the ugliest forest but we are the happiest forest in the whole world!”

All the other trees and animals of the forest were one happy family once again.

The End

Michael Pellico, Author

Michael Pellico is a medical researcher, writer, and film producer. One of eleven children whose parents both worked long hours. It was his responsibility to help raise his siblings. Growing up "poor", he entertained them with stories, and later telling stories to their children. This book and all his stories are dedicated to Sabrina, his niece, who insists that he tell her a story each time they are together. We hope that you love them as much as Sabrina does!

Malane Newman, Illustrator

Malane Newman is a professional freelance illustrator and cartoonist. Born and raised in San Diego, she grew up with a passion for cartoon illustration. She is self-taught and began as a traditional cartoonist and evolved to illustrating on computer many years ago. She is a master at creating eye candy with color and illustrates in many different cartooning styles. She has worked on famous properties like Barbie and Swan Princess. Her work has appeared on food and product packaging, board games, children's books, greeting cards, and other consumer products. We hope you love her art as much as she enjoyed creating it!